My
Little Book of
MANNERS

This book belongs to:

_____

Published by Sequoia Children's Publishing,
a division of Phoenix International Publications, Inc.

8501 West Higgins Road, Suite 790   59 Gloucester Place
Chicago, Illinois 60631   London W1U 8JJ

www.sequoiakidsbooks.com

10 9 8 7 6 5 4 3 2 1

ISBN 978-1-64269-072-9

Contents

Please and Thank You 5

In the Bathroom 13

Good Manners 22

Play Nice 37

A Helping Hand 46

Be Patient 54

Let's Be Friends 72

Table Manners 90

Excuse Me 98

I'm Sorry 104

Be Honest 120

Let's Share 132

Goops 142

Please and Thank You

Illustrated by Gabriele Antonini

Karl Kitten was in a hurry. He had come to the toy store to buy a birthday present for his good friend, Boris Bunny. There were so many toys to choose from. Boris liked games and Boris liked sports, too, so Karl decided to give him a ball.

The trouble was that Karl didn't know where the ball section was in this particular toy store.

Karl found a worker. "Will you please show me where you keep the balls?" Karl asked.

"I'd be happy to be of assistance," said the friendly worker. "The balls are right here."

Karl saw shelf after shelf of different balls. There were big balls and little balls.

There were colorful balls and bouncy balls.

"I'd like that ball with the stars on it, please," said Karl.

Thank you

Karl Kitten took the ball home. Now he had to wrap the present so he could take it to Boris Bunny's birthday party.

Karl put the ball in a box and began to cover the box with wrapping paper. It was a very big job and Karl was having a lot of trouble.

"Would you like some help?" Karl's mother asked him.

"Yes, please," said Karl.

Working together, Karl and his mother wrapped the gift. Karl's mother even helped him wrap the box with a pretty ribbon and tie the ribbon into a really neat bow.

Please and Thank You

"Thank you for your help," said Karl.

"You're welcome," said Karl's mother. "Thank you for using such nice manners."

Karl's mother gave her little kitten a big hug. Soon it would be time for Karl to go to the big birthday party.

Karl arrived at the Bunny family's house. He carried the gift.

"Thank you for coming, Karl," said Mr. Bunny.

Soon it was time for cake. Karl and the other friends sang "Happy Birthday" to Boris. Boris blew out his candles.

Mrs. Bunny began to serve the friends plates of birthday cake.

"Thank you for the cake," said Karl.

"May I have a big piece, please?" asked Percy Puppy.

"Certainly," said Mrs. Bunny. "I hope you enjoy it."

All of the friends did enjoy eating the birthday cake.

Please and Thank You

After everyone had finished eating their cake, it was time for Boris to open his presents.

"Presents are the best thing about birthdays!" Boris said. His friends agreed with him.

Boris began to open the gift that Karl brought. "You did a nice job wrapping this," Boris said.

"Thank you," said Karl. "My mom helped me."

"It's a bouncy ball!" said Boris. "Thank you so much. I've always wanted one of these."

"You're welcome," said Karl.

Boris's friends watched as he opened the rest of his presents. He got many exciting new toys.

"Thank you all for coming to my party," Boris said. "And thank you for all of these great gifts!"

"Thank you for inviting us," said his friends.

It had been a very nice birthday — made even better by using nice manners.

In the Bathroom

Illustrated by Tim Warren

It was a bright morning. Percy Panda woke up, all set to get ready for his first day of school.

"Good morning, Percy," said Percy's father.

"Good morning, Papa," said Percy.

Papa Panda stood in the bathroom wearing his bathrobe. He was brushing his teeth before he shaved and took a shower. Percy liked watching his father rub shaving cream all over his face. Someday he would be able to shave, too.

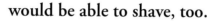

"Here's your toothbrush," said Papa Panda, handing Percy his toothbrush with toothpaste on it. "Be sure to brush your teeth really well."

Percy brushed the teeth in front. He brushed the teeth far in the back. He even brushed his tongue.

In the Bathroom

"Now that your teeth are brushed, you need to take a bath before school," said Papa Panda.

Percy loved bath time.

Papa Panda filled the tub with warm water.

While water gushed out of the faucet, Percy poured bubble bath into the tub. Soon it was full of suds and Percy climbed in.

Quack!

Percy squeezed his rubber duck and it quacked a squeaky quack.

While Papa Panda watched, Percy played in the tub. Bath time sure was a lot of fun!

"Now it's time to wash," said Papa Panda. He handed Percy some shampoo and a bar of soap.

Percy lathered himself with the soap. Soon his whole body was covered with soap suds. He rubbed and scrubbed until the soap washed away all of the dirt. Then Percy squeezed a little shampoo onto the top of his head and washed his hair.

Soon he was all finished — and all clean!

After his bath, Percy Panda needed to go to the bathroom. "I've gotta go," Percy told his papa.

Papa Panda dried Percy off and then lifted his son onto the toilet.

Percy waited and waited. He had needed to use the bathroom just a minute before, but now he couldn't go. So he sat on the toilet and waited.

Percy sang a little song as he sat.

"Potty, potty, panda's on the potty," he sang. "Why can't Percy Panda use the potty?"

Pretty soon, however, Percy was able to go.

"I'm very proud of you, son," said Papa Panda. "Using the big toilet is a sign that you're really growing up."

Percy was glad that his father was so proud of him. And he was glad that he'd been able to go.

Once Percy was finished on the toilet, he took some toilet tissue. He wiped himself and made sure he was good and clean.

In the Bathroom

After Percy was done on the toilet, there was something else that he needed to do.

"Be sure to wash your hands," said Papa Panda.

Using soap and warm water, Percy washed his hands.

Hand washing is very important. Whether it is after you use the bathroom, when you finish playing outside, or before a meal, washing your hands with soap and water is a habit worth having.

Germs and dirt and other things stick to the skin on your hands. You don't want those germs and dirt getting into your mouth or getting onto others. So when you are done playing or pottying, and before you eat, be sure to wash those hands.

Washing his hands hadn't been the only thing Percy Panda had done in the bathroom. He had brushed his teeth to keep them shiny and healthy.

He had taken a bath, washing his body and shampooing his hair. And he had gone to the bathroom, something that everyone does.

The bathroom had been a busy part of Percy's morning. And doing all his bathroom things left Percy feeling clean and healthy and ready for the rest of his day.

Good Manners

Illustrated by Lance Raichert

Good Manners

It is the start of a new school day for Ms. Hen and her students. "Good morning, class," Ms. Hen says. "Aren't we all full of talk and laughter today!"

But Ms. Hen's students are so busy talking that they do not hear her. Ms. Hen begins the day by reading a book to her class. Puppy and his friends can barely sit still through the whole story.

After reading, Ms. Hen turns to the chalkboard and begins the day's math lesson. "We're going to learn all about addition," she says.

Ms. Hen shows a math problem on the board, but nobody pays attention. They're all busy listening to Pig tell a funny joke.

Ms. Hen turns from the chalkboard. "Talking when it is not your turn to talk is not nice," she says. "Does anyone know what rude means?" The class grows silent. They know Ms. Hen is unhappy with them.

"It's when you don't use good manners," says Puppy.

"Yes," says Ms. Hen. "And good manners are when you wait to be called on before you speak in class. Having good manners means saying please and thank you to your friends. Good manners are when you treat others how you would like to be treated."

The students all wish they had used good manners that morning. They wish they had listened to Ms. Hen when she was teaching.

As the class begins its science lesson, Ms. Hen thinks her students have learned their lesson about using good manners. "Today we will be conducting a new science experiment," she says. "You will all need to listen very carefully to my instructions."

Ms. Hen shows the students how to make flowers change colors. Everyone is so excited to do the experiment that they forget to use good manners.

"I'm going to use red!" says Mouse. "It's so pretty!"

"Blue is my favorite color," says Hippo.

Good Manners

"Catch this!" Skunk says as he throws a paper airplane through the air to Puppy.

Ms. Hen gets an idea for a new experiment, one that will teach a lesson about good manners.

"For our next experiment," says Ms. Hen, "I want you all to forget about using good manners for the rest of the school day."

Puppy and his friends can hardly believe what they are hearing!

"This is going to be the best experiment!" says Cat.

"No saying please and thank you for me!" says Pig.

"I won't share with anyone," Turtle says.

"And I will talk whenever I want to," says Bear.

Skunk isn't sure about the experiment, though. He worries that his friends will be mean to each other.

Ms. Hen knows that bad manners will make teaching very hard. But she thinks the lesson her students will learn about good manners is very important.

Good Manners

The bell rings for recess. Ms. Hen's students jump up and rush outside. Usually, Ms. Hen's students are not allowed to push and run to the door. But in the spirit of her good manners experiment, Ms. Hen just watches them push and shove each other as they run outside.

"Look out!" says Hippo as he pushes past his classmates. "I may be slow, but I sure am big!"

"Hey!" Pig yells. "That's not fair!"

"Wait your turn, Hippo!" shouts Cat.

Pig and Cat want to be the first ones on the playground, but Hippo squeezes out the door instead. The rest of the class stampedes to the door after them.

Ms. Hen lets the students use bad manners. She just sits and grades the papers on her desk.

Good Manners

Once everyone is on the playground, Puppy tries to organize a fun game for them to play.

"I want to show you all a new game," Puppy says.

"Why don't we play baseball?" shouts Mouse.

"I think we should play kickball," says Hippo.

"But I want to play dodgeball," whines Cat.

"Why don't we play baseball?" shouts Mouse, jumping up and down.

"I don't want to play any of those silly games," snorts Pig. "I want to play hide-and-seek." With that, he runs off to hide, even though none of his friends have agreed to play his game.

The others are so busy arguing that they don't even realize Pig has left. They're so busy bickering, in fact, that recess is over before they can choose a game at all.

Good Manners

Back in the classroom, the students settle in for reading time. It is Hippo's turn to read today. He is very excited to share his favorite story with his friends.

"Once upon a time, a king lived in a castle…" Hippo begins to read.

But Hippo's friends do not pay much attention to his story. Instead, they talk to each other.

"If I were a king I would have a castle made of candy," says Puppy.

"I would be your court jester and make you laugh," chuckles Pig.

"I would be a beautiful princess," says Mouse. Ms. Hen feels sorry for Hippo. If his friends were using good manners, they would pay attention to him.

Good Manners

Once reading is done, Ms. Hen thinks her students have learned their lesson.

"Now that the day is nearly over," she says, "I am curious to know what you thought of my experiment."

Cat is the first one to raise her hand. Ms. Hen nods to her and Cat speaks. "I didn't think it was very nice when Hippo pushed me before recess."

Puppy raises his hand, too. He waits until Ms. Hen calls on him to speak. "Recess wasn't any fun at all," he says. "We didn't even get to play because no one could agree on a game."

Hippo raises his hand. "My friends made me feel bad when they didn't listen to me read. I know how you feel when we talk while you try to teach," he tells Ms. Hen.

Good Manners

"So what did these experiences teach you about good manners?" Ms. Hen asks her class.

"I learned that when you use good manners, you think of others before yourself," says Mouse.

"I learned that without good manners, no one would listen to anyone else," says Bunny.

Finally, Ms. Hen adds, "Don't you all agree that learning is much harder when the class is loud and you all talk at once?"

"Oh, yes!" the students all say.

When the school bell rings, the class waits to be dismissed and stands in a nice, straight line. As Hippo lets his friends go first, Ms. Hen watches. She knows good manners won't be a problem again.

Play Nice

Illustrated by Tim Warren

The sun shone brightly down on the schoolyard. Birds chirped. Flowers bloomed. Balls bounced and rolled. The laughter of children's voices filled the air. It was time for recess!

Katie Kitten ran to play with her friends.

Some of them kicked balls. Katie wanted to try. "May I play ball with you?" she asked.

"Sure thing," said Tommy Cat.

Katie was glad that her friends shared their toys and games with her. Sharing was a big part of playing nice. And playing nice made recess lots of fun.

Play Nice

At the other end of the sandbox, three friends were busy building a sand castle.

Martha Mouse filled a pail with sand. With each pail of sand, Martha built another part of the sand castle.

With the help of her friends playing nicely with her, Martha Mouse was able to finish her sand castle before recess was over.

Play Nice

Elsewhere in the schoolyard, other children were not having so much fun. Katie Kitten heard yelling. The yelling voice was saying some very mean and hurtful things. Katie Kitten also heard someone crying.

Katie walked until she saw where the yelling and crying were coming from.

"You're little like a baby!" yelled Wally Wolf. He was yelling at poor Rebecca Rabbit.

"Why are you so mean to me?" Rebecca asked.

"Because I don't like you!" said Wally.

He sure was being mean. Rebecca cried and cried.

Katie walked up to Wally. "That's no way to talk to someone," she said. "It's not nice to yell at people and hurt their feelings. Nobody likes a bully."

Play Nice

"I guess I hadn't thought about it that way," said Wally. "I don't want to be a bully."

Wally apologized to Rebecca and the two began to play together nicely.

The school bell rang. Recess was over.

The children walked and ran back to the school. There, they lined up in straight lines. It was time to go back inside to learn.

"I sure had fun at recess," said Harold Hare.

"Me, too," said Henrietta Hog. "Recess is my favorite part of the day."

"Mine, too," said Marty Monkey. "But learning and doing things inside is great, too."

Play Nice

As the children walked politely back into the school, their teacher, Mr. Snout, asked them how their recess had been.

"Playing nice helps make it so much fun," said Penelope Penguin.

"That is very true," Mr. Snout said. "I'm so very proud of how nicely I saw you children playing today. Way to behave!"

A Helping Hand

Illustrated by Tim Warren

It was a beautiful summer day, and Polly Puppy headed into the neighborhood for a walk. The birds were chirping. The sun was shining, and Polly's neighbors and friends were all outside, too.

As Polly walked down the sidewalk, Mrs. Cow was leaving a store. Mrs. Cow was pushing her baby in a stroller.

"Let me hold the door for you," said Polly.

"Why, thank you," said Mrs. Cow. "That was very kind of you. What a big help you are!"

A Helping Hand

As Polly continued on her walk, she saw her father, Officer Puppy. He was directing traffic and making sure everyone stayed safe—whether they were walking or driving.

"Hi, Daddy!" said Polly. "Guess what? I've been helping other people today—just like you do!"

"I'm so proud of you, Polly," her father said.

"When I grow up, I want to be a police officer, just like you," Polly said.

"Well, keep helping others and you'll be well on your way," said Officer Puppy.

Soon Polly had another chance to help someone. She saw old Mrs. Whiskers walking across the street.

Mrs. Whiskers walked with the help of a cane. She walked very slowly.

"Let me give you a hand," said Polly.

She helped Mrs. Whiskers safely to the other side of the street.

"You are such a good helper, Polly," said Mrs. Whiskers. "Thank you for helping me cross the street safely!"

"You're welcome, Mrs. Whiskers!" said Polly. "Have a nice day!"

A Helping Hand

Farther down the sidewalk, Polly spotted her friend Huey Hippo.

"Hi, Huey," Polly said.

"Hey there, Polly," said Huey. "I lost my pet frog. I'm putting up posters so people know to look for it."

"I'll give you a hand," said Polly. "With the two of us looking, I bet we'll find your frog." Polly was a very good seeker and finder.

She looked in trees and behind houses. She looked beneath rocks. Soon she found Huey's frog hiding behind a trash bin.

"Thanks for your help, Polly," Huey said. "I couldn't have found my frog without you."

At the end of the day, Polly was very happy. She was happy that she'd been able to help so many friends and neighbors.

As Polly walked home, she stopped by the playground. Sitting all alone on the swing was her little brother, Percy.

"Hi, Percy," said Polly.

"Hi, Polly," said Percy. "I need a push. Could you give me one, please?"

"Sure thing," said Polly. Lending a helping hand was something she was good at—and something she loved doing.

A Helping Hand

Be Patient

Illustrated by Lance Raichert

Be Patient

One sunny summer day, Puppy leaves his house early. He is going to the park to meet his friends. He hops on his tricycle and pedals down the street.

Puppy's little trike is getting old. The paint is fading, and it has one wobbly wheel in back. That wobbly wheel makes his tricycle hard to ride. It really slows Puppy down.

Puppy is getting too big for his little trike. When he was smaller, the tricycle was just the right size for him. But Puppy is growing.

Every time Puppy pedals, his legs keep hitting the handlebars! That really slows Puppy down.

Puppy pedals as fast as he can, but he never goes very fast. He huffs and puffs, but he hardly gets anywhere at all!

Puppy walks the rest of the way to the park. He pulls his old tricycle along behind him.

At last Puppy arrives at the park. His friends are already there, riding their bicycles along the paths.

"What took you so long?" his friends ask.

"I left early," answers Puppy, "but I'm still the last one here!"

Puppy's friends take one look at Puppy's wobbly little tricycle. Then they know what took him so long.

Hippo stops by on his big bike. Hippo was Puppy's first friend to have a two-wheeler. "I remember when I outgrew my tricycle," Hippo says. "I'd get on, and no matter how hard I pedaled, I couldn't make it go."

"That's what happened to me," says Puppy. "It took me forever to ride two blocks!"

"You should start thinking about getting a new bike," says Hippo.

Be Patient

Be Patient

"Everyone else has two-wheelers now."

Pig and Cat zoom by on their speedy bikes. They ring their handlebar bells at Puppy. "See you after the race!" they call to him.

Puppy cannot join a race with his old tricycle, and he cannot play with his friends as long as they ride their bikes all day! Puppy is really feeling left out. He pulls his trike away from the park.

"These bikes all cost so much!" Puppy says, his breath fogging up the bicycle shop window. "I don't have enough money to buy one!"

Puppy does not need a fancy racing bike. He just wants a simple two-wheeler. He could even do without a bell on the handlebars.

"Bell or no bell," he sighs, "these bikes still cost way too much!"

Feeling sad, Puppy walks home, pulling his tricycle behind him.

Puppy walks by the bicycle shop every day for a week. He stops to stare in the window. He looks at the price tags, but he could never afford a new bike.

Puppy has been saving his allowance, but he would have to save for a very long time before he had enough money to buy a new bike.

"I'll never get a two-wheeler," Puppy says to himself.

One day, Hippo sees a very sad Puppy staring at a red bike in the window of the bike shop. "Are you going to get a new two-wheeler?" Hippo asks.

"I don't have enough money," Puppy answers. "I hardly have enough for a set of training wheels!"

"Why don't you get those now?" Hippo suggests. "They will remind you to keep saving money until you have enough to buy the rest of the bike!"

"That's a great idea!" says Puppy. "I'll do it!"

Puppy saves his money for weeks and weeks, but he still has not saved enough to buy a new bike.

Puppy is feeling lonely all summer long. Most days, his friends like to ride to the park. When they do, they leave Puppy behind.

60

Be Patient

Puppy feels a little bit better a few weeks later. It is his favorite time of year. His birthday is just around the corner! His friends always plan a big party for him.

When the big day comes, though, nobody says a word about it! Puppy expects to receive a few little gifts from his friends. Instead, Puppy just gets bad news.

"We're riding to the park," says Hippo. "We'll see you later."

As he walks slowly back home, Puppy says, "This is the worst birthday ever!"

But when he gets to his house, his friends are there to greet him. "Surprise!" they shout. And they wheel out his birthday gift.

"A new bike!" Puppy says. "You guys are the best! This is the greatest birthday ever! But how did you have enough money to buy me a new bike?"

"It's not really new," says Hippo. "It used to belong to Bear's older brother."

Be Patient

"He got too big for it," Bear explains. "But we fixed it up for you so it's as good as new!"

"It's new to me!" Puppy exclaims. "I can't wait to ride it!"

Hippo helps Puppy put his training wheels on the new two-wheeler.

Then they are off for Puppy's first ride with his friends in a long time.

"We'll race you to the park!" says Pig, zooming ahead. Puppy pedals as fast as he can, but he is still getting used to the big new bike. Puppy is the last one to arrive at the park.

"What took you so long?" laughs Pig. "Are those baby wheels slowing you down?"

Puppy feels sad. He parks his birthday gift in the bike rack and watches his friends zoom by him.

Be Patient

Hippo stops to see what is wrong.

"Do you have a flat tire, or what?" asks Hippo. "Come ride with us!"

"I can't keep up with you," Puppy sighs. "Not with these training wheels."

Hippo and Cat offer to pedal more slowly, but Puppy does not want them to slow down for him. Pig would only make fun of them.

"I am a year older now," Puppy says. "I want to ride as fast as everyone else!" Puppy knows it is not that easy. It takes practice to learn to ride a two-wheeler.

"One ride with training wheels is not enough," says Hippo. "You have to get used to a taller bike."

Hippo uses his own bike to show Puppy a few important things about riding a two-wheeler.

Be Patient

"You can put your leg down if you feel like you're falling," Hippo says.

Puppy does not want to fall over. He practices a bit with the training wheels. The next day, Hippo is waiting for him at the bike rack.

"I remembered how I learned to ride without training wheels," Hippo says. "The best way to learn is to try it! And if you're ready, I'll show you how."

Puppy is still a little bit scared that he will fall over. But he really wants to go faster.

"I'm ready!" says Puppy.

Together, Puppy and Hippo take off the training wheels. Puppy feels shaky when he climbs on the seat. He feels like he is tipping over, but Hippo helps to hold the bike up. "You take care of the pedaling and steering," says Hippo, "and I'll hold the bike up straight."

While Puppy pedals slowly, Hippo runs alongside him.

Be Patient

Puppy pumps the pedals as fast as he can. He likes to feel the wind on his fur!

"Am I going too fast for you, Hippo?" Puppy asks.

Hippo does not answer. He is not holding onto the bike anymore! Hippo let go when Puppy started pedaling quickly. Puppy has been riding a two-wheeler all by himself!

"I knew you could do it!" Hippo calls. Puppy finds Hippo in the crowd of his friends. He is waving at Puppy.

"Now come back!" Hippo calls. "Just keep pedaling until you get here!" Puppy rides toward his friends. Even Pig cheers him on.

Puppy keeps the bike up the whole ride back. He also remembers to use his leg when he stops, just like Hippo taught him to do.

"Congratulations on your first solo ride!" says Hippo.

"I've never ridden so fast before!" Puppy says. "But I didn't do it myself. You helped me learn how!"

Be Patient

Let's Be Friends

Illustrated by Lance Raichert

Let's Be Friends

It is almost time for morning recess in Ms. Hen's busy classroom. The students have spent the morning reading, writing, and learning new spelling words.

Everyone is sitting quietly, waiting to be dismissed. It is a sunny day, and Puppy has stared out the window many times this morning.

Puppy sits up straight and looks like he is paying attention, but he is really thinking about what fun it will be to play tag with his friends at recess.

Bunny is thinking up a new dance she wants to try out on the playground. Pig wants to try a daring new trick on the jungle gym. Mouse hopes to play hide-and-seek. It is her favorite game to play at recess.

When everyone has stopped fidgeting, Ms. Hen says, "All right, class. You may walk in a line quietly down the hall and go out to recess. Enjoy yourselves! I'll be out in a few minutes."

Puppy leads the small parade quietly down the long hallway. As soon as the students go out the double doors to the playground, they start to run and shout and play.

Bunny does a lively dance. "I like to call this dance the Playground Polka," she says.

"Look at me!" shouts Pig. He is hanging by his knees from the high bars of the jungle gym and swinging back and forth. He is happy to perform for an audience.

Everyone is so busy watching Pig that they do not see the new student who goes into the school all by himself.

Let's Be Friends

The new student's name is Skunk. He watches all of the friends play, and hopes that they will like him. Skunk really wants to make new friends at his new school.

Skunk looks at the note in his hand. It has a 3 written on it. He finds the door with a number three on it, and walks into Ms. Hen's classroom.

Ms. Hen is on her way to watch the students on the playground when she sees Skunk standing there.

"My goodness!" clucks Ms. Hen. "If it isn't the new student! We were just about to get ready for you. Here is your new desk, right next to Puppy's desk. And here is the cubby for your lunch box."

Skunk looks around the bright classroom and smiles. Ms. Hen makes him feel welcome.

Let's Be Friends

"The other students are playing outside," says Ms. Hen, showing Skunk to the playground. "Why don't you go join them for the rest of recess? I'll get your desk set up with books, pencils, paper, and scissors."

On the playground, Skunk sees the other children playing, but he is too shy to join in.

Skunk is relieved that no one notices him. He stays hidden by the bushes at the edge of the playground. Safe in his hiding spot, Skunk is able to watch his new classmates play.

The sunlight makes shadows in the bushes. With his bright white stripe on his back, this makes Skunk very hard to see. He is able to watch the other students play without them even noticing him.

Let's Be Friends

Suddenly, Skunk feels a funny tickle on the bottom of his foot. A moment later, he feels a sharp poke.

"Ouch!" Skunk says, lifting up his foot to rub it.

Just then, Mouse scurries out of a hole that Skunk hadn't even noticed.

Mouse runs a safe distance away from Skunk, then turns and says, "You scared me! Your foot blocked the hole I was hiding in."

"I'm sorry," Skunk says. "I didn't see the hole. I was just sitting down to watch the kids play. I'm new here. This is my first day of school."

"Well, why didn't you say so?" says Mouse. "I'll show you around."

Let's Be Friends

"Let's walk over to the jungle gym and I'll introduce you to Pig," says Mouse.

Skunk smiles and heads over to the jungle gym.

"Hey, kid," Pig calls to Skunk. "Do you want to see the great trick I can do?"

"Sure," says Skunk.

Pig swings back and forth by his knees.

"That is great!" says Skunk.

"Why don't you try it?" Pig says.

"Pig, this is Skunk, the new kid in our class," Mouse says. "I'm showing him around."

Skunk climbs onto the jungle gym and hangs on the bars next to Pig.

"It's nice to have you here, Skunk," says Pig.

Let's Be Friends

Suddenly Bunny hops along. She does a twirling leap and lands underneath the jungle gym, directly below Pig and Skunk.

"Hello, down there!" say Pig and Skunk, clapping at Bunny's acrobatic show.

Bunny curtsies and says, "Hello, Pig! I was dancing the Playground Polka." But then she jumps backward, startled at seeing the striped new kid.

"I don't think you've had a chance to meet the new kid," says Pig. "His name is Skunk."

"Well, it's nice to meet you, Skunk," Bunny says. "Do you like dancing?"

"I've never tried," says Skunk.

Pig and Skunk grab the bars and drop to the ground.

Let's Be Friends

85

As the two land on their feet, Puppy dashes past them. He is running all over the playground, jumping over imaginary logs and puddles, when he hears his friends laughing. With a big smile on his face, Puppy runs around them before coming to a stop.

"Whew! That was fun!" says Puppy.

Pig steps forward and says, "Puppy, we have a new kid at school. We'd all like you to meet Skunk."

"It's great to have a new kid in our class," says Puppy.

"It sure is," says Mouse. "Especially one with such a neat-looking stripe."

"Who appreciates talent!" says Pig.

"Who might like dancing!" says Bunny.

"It's great to be here," Skunk says to his new friends.

Let's Be Friends

"I have an idea," says Puppy. "Let's think of a game we can all play. What game do you want to play, Skunk?"

"How about a game of tag?" Skunk asks.

The friends all giggle and run around the playground. Skunk is beginning to feel like he fits in. He really likes all of his new friends.

Soon Ms. Hen blows her whistle. The classmates all line up and march quietly into the classroom.

"Thank you for playing tag with me," Skunk says.

"Why wouldn't we?" Puppy says. "You're part of our class now. We can finish our game tomorrow at recess."

Ms. Hen smiles. "Well done, class," she says. "And well done, Skunk. It's good to see that you made friends all by yourselves."

Let's Be Friends

Table Manners

Illustrated by Hannah Wood

Table Manners

Mama Dog's voice rang from the house. "Come to the table. It's time for dinner."

Dolly, Davy, and Doug raced inside and into the dining room. A day of playing had made them rather hungry—and dinner smelled delicious!

"My favorite!"said Davy. "Peas and mashed potatoes!"

Mama Dog saw her puppies' dirty paws.

"Go wash up, please," she said.

After washing their paws, the puppies came to the dinner table. They sat down in their chairs and placed their napkins on their laps, just as Mama Dog had taught them to do.

"This sure smells great, Mama," said Dolly.
She couldn't wait to eat.

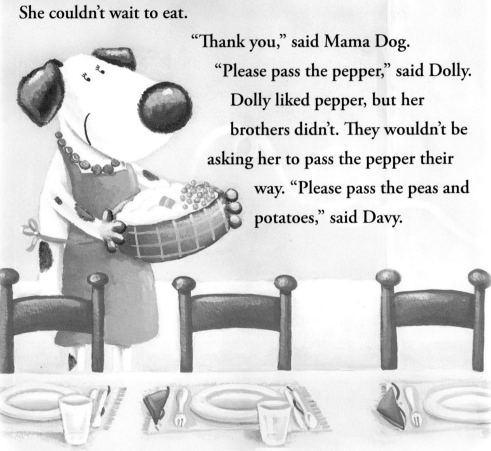

"Thank you," said Mama Dog.

"Please pass the pepper," said Dolly.
Dolly liked pepper, but her
brothers didn't. They wouldn't be
asking her to pass the pepper their
way. "Please pass the peas and
potatoes," said Davy.

92

Doug, who was the youngest and smallest of the three puppies, passed the bowl of food to his brother. He was glad that Davy had asked so politely.

Davy took a spoonful of peas and a dollop of potatoes and plopped them down onto his plate. Then he passed the bowl back to Doug, who hadn't gotten any yet.

"Please pass the peas and potatoes to me when you're finished," said Dolly.

As polite as the puppies had been so far, they soon forgot their table manners. Instead of sitting like nice little puppies, using their forks and spoons, and behaving as Mama Dog expected, they began to act as if they were raised by wolves!

"Mah blah vah fah blah," Davy said, his mouth full of food. No one understood what he was trying to say.

"Whoopee!" said Dolly, watching a pea fly from her fork and across the table.

Doug didn't understand why his brother and sister were behaving so badly. Mama Dog had taught them never to talk with food in their mouths.

Table Manners

Not only was it rude, but it was unsafe, as well. And Mama always said not to play with your food.

Mama saw how the two puppies were behaving and asked them to stop. "Were you born in a barn?" she asked.

Doug thought that was funny.

Dolly and Davy finally began to eat like nice, mannerly puppies. Their dinner was very delicious. Peas weren't Davy's favorite, but he knew they were healthy. So he hid a few peas in each bite of potatoes — and he could hardly even taste them!

Dolly hurried to finish her dinner because what came after dinner was the best part. That was when Mama Dog served the puppies their dessert! Dolly was finishing the last of her peas when she heard Doug's voice.

Table Manners

"I'm finished," said Doug. "May I be excused, please?" The littlest puppy cleared his place and carried his dishes to the kitchen sink. What a polite little puppy he was!

"You've behaved very nicely," said Mama Dog. "Doug, you may have the first helping of dessert. It's your favorite—orange sherbet!"

Doug was glad for dessert. But most of all, he was happy that Mama Dog was so proud of his good table manners.

Excuse Me

Illustrated by Gabrielle Antonini

Excuse Me

The Critterville Theater was where everyone went to watch movies. The movie theater was always playing lots of movies. There were funny movies and sweet movies. There were exciting movies and even spooky movies. There was always something for everyone to enjoy.

One evening Heather Heifer and her mother decided to see a movie at the theater. There were many movies to choose from.

But they weren't sure where to go. Heather saw two ushers who could help them.

"Excuse me," Heather said. "My mother and I were wondering which theater is showing the new Moo-lia Roberts movie."

"It's the second door on the right," said one of the ushers.

"Thank you," said Heather.

The theater showing their movie was already very crowded. It seemed as if quite a few folks wanted to see this particular film. Heather and her mother looked for two empty seats where they could sit.

"There are two seats right there," said Heather's mother, however, someone was sitting in a seat that blocked their path.

"Excuse me," said Heather. "I was wondering if my mother and I could get through. We'd like to sit in those two seats."

"No problem," said the friendly penguin.

Excuse Me

Soon the lights in the theater dimmed. The big movie screen was filled with dazzling pictures. The movie was beginning!

Everyone sat quietly, ready to watch the movie. Everyone, that is, except Ben Boa and Glenn Grizzly. The two friends kept talking even though the movie had started. They laughed and talked very loudly.

Because of Ben and Glenn's loud talking and laughing, others in the theater were having trouble hearing the movie.

"Excuse me," said Mrs. Heifer. "Would you two please keep it down? There are many people who want to enjoy this fine movie."

"We're sorry," said Benjamin Boa. "We didn't realize we were bugging you. We'll be quiet for the rest of the movie."

Glenn Grizzly was a bit embarrassed by his own behavior. His parents had always taught him to use nice manners. He would remember to use those manners from now on.

Everyone in the theater was now able to enjoy the movie in peace. They laughed. They cried. They all had a very nice time.

The movie was nearly over. Everyone was watching to see how it ended. Suddenly, Heather felt a tickle in her nose and sneezed.

"Excuse me," whispered Heather. She felt awful for making such a loud noise.

"Bless you," whispered her mother. "See? It's okay to sneeze—if you remember your manners."

I'm Sorry

Illustrated by Lance Raichert

One bright morning, Cat is playing in the park. She is jumping and skipping, chasing a beautiful butterfly. "Come back, butterfly!" she calls.

As Cat hops along, one of her best friends hops onto the path in front of her. It's Bunny!

"Good morning, Cat!" Bunny says.

"Hello, Bunny!" says Cat. "What are you doing here in the park?"

"I'm practicing my dance moves," says Bunny. "I call this dance the Bunny Hop."

Cat dances along, following Bunny all the way home. When they reach Bunny's front porch, Cat says, "You're such a good dancer, Bunny. I wish I could dance like you."

"Thank you," says Bunny. "If you practice like I do, you could dance like me. Would you like to come inside?"

Bunny twirls around and leads Cat to her bedroom. There, next to Bunny's bed, are her special dancing shoes. Cat has an idea.

"Bunny, can I ask you a favor?" Cat says shyly. "Would you let me borrow your dancing shoes for a few days?"

"How come?" Bunny asks.

"I really do want to dance like you," Cat says. "And I think it will help a lot if I wear your dancing shoes while I practice."

"I don't know," says Bunny. "When I practice, I always wear my dancing shoes. I'd hate to be without them."

"Please!" begs Cat. "I know they'll make me better!"

I'm Sorry

"But," Bunny says, "you don't always return the things you borrow."

"That's only because sometimes things get lost," says Cat. "That's not my fault."

"But it is your fault when things get lost," says Bunny. "If you took care of things, they might not get misplaced."

"I promise I'll take good care of your dancing shoes," Cat says. "Will you please let me borrow them?"

Cat makes so many promises that Bunny finally lets her borrow the special shoes.

"Don't wear these shoes outside," Bunny says. "They are only for indoors."

But Cat isn't even listening. She is already dancing home to try the special dancing shoes.

I'm Sorry

Later, Mouse comes over to Cat's house to play.

"Correct me if I'm wrong," says Mouse, "but aren't those Bunny's special dancing shoes?"

"Yes, they are," says Cat. "Bunny let me borrow them so that I can practice. Don't they fit me perfectly?"

With that, Cat does a dance for Mouse.

Mouse watches her friend dance, surprised that Bunny let Cat borrow her shoes.

"I call this dance the Catwalk," Cat says as she dances across her bedroom floor, flinging scarves and other colorful clothing through the air like banners.

"Well, you don't dance like Bunny," says Mouse. "But I really like your way of dancing, too. The Catwalk is a great new dance!"

I'm Sorry

The next day, Cat decides to practice the Catwalk even more. Cat is busy looking all around her room for Bunny's dancing shoes when she hears a knock at the front door.

When Cat opens the door, she is surprised to see Bunny standing there.

"Hi, Bunny," says Cat. "I'm having a great time with your shoes. You don't need them back yet, do you?"

"Well," says Bunny, "I really need them back now. And I'd love to see you dance. Mouse says you're pretty good!"

"Of course," says Cat. She leaves Bunny outside and goes to her room to look again. But Bunny's dance shoes are nowhere to be found.

"I'm sorry, Bunny," Cat says. "I can't find them."

I'm Sorry

Bunny walks home sadly and slowly. When she gets home, Mouse is there waiting for her.

"Hi, Bunny," says Mouse. "What's wrong?"

"I just went to Cat's house to get my dancing shoes," Bunny says. "She told me they're lost. I shouldn't have let her borrow them."

"I've seen Cat's room," says Mouse. "It's very messy."

"I know," says Bunny, "but how will that help me find my shoes?"

"I have an idea!" says Mouse. "I'll help Cat clean her room. Maybe that way I can find your shoes."

"That's a great idea," Bunny says, "but I'll help you clean. They're my shoes, after all."

With that, the friends head to Cat's house.

I'm Sorry

Mouse and Bunny find Cat sitting on her front porch, looking sad.

"Hello, Cat," Mouse says with a serious voice. "We've come to help you clean your room so we can find Bunny's dancing shoes."

"But I've already looked everywhere," says Cat. "It's hopeless. The shoes are lost."

"But now you have some help," says Mouse. "Come on, Cat. Come on, Bunny. Don't mope. Let's get to work!"

In Cat's room, Mouse says, "Let's find a good place to put everything away. Like clothes in the closet."

"And books on the bookself," says Bunny.

"And toys in the toy box," says Mouse.

After lots of hard work, Cat's room begins to look tidy. There is only one pile of clothes left to put away.

I'm Sorry

Cat picks up the clothes one by one, while Mouse and Bunny put them away.

Suddenly, Cat shouts, "Bunny! Here are your shoes!"

"I knew we would find them!" Mouse cheers.

"Thank you!" says Bunny. "I'm so glad to have my special dancing shoes back."

"I'm sorry," says Cat. "I didn't mean to lose them."

"I know," Bunny says, giving Cat a hug. "And now that your room is tidy, you'll know where your things are!"

Bunny, Cat, and Mouse walk outside into the warm sunshine. They dance happily together.

"Let's call this dance The Happy Ending!" Cat says.

I'm Sorry

Be Honest

Illustrated by Lance Raichert

Be Honest

Gym class on the playground is one of the best parts of the day for Puppy and his friends. Today they are playing kickball. The game is close, but Puppy isn't worried because it is Hippo's turn to kick.

"We need a good kick, Hippo," Puppy calls. "I know you can do it!"

With one swing of his strong leg, Hippo sends the ball flying! It bounces to the fence while Hippo runs around the bases. Hippo may

be the best kicker, but he is not a fast runner. It will be a very close call at home base.

Hippo slides into home. When the dust clears, Puppy's team starts to cheer. Hippo won the game! Puppy and his teammates are champions for the day!

The friends charge back to the classroom. They are still cheering about Hippo's home run.

Skunk had missed the game, so his friends tell him all about it.

"You should have seen Hippo's home run!" says Cat.

"Hippo won the game!" Puppy says.

"The best part of it was when I slid into home on my belly!" Hippo says. "Here, I'll show you how I did it."

Hippo runs to the front of the classroom. He takes three huge steps and dives to the floor.

But inside Ms. Hen's classroom, there isn't much space for big slides. Hippo bumps into Ms. Hen's desk. Before Hippo can stop it, Ms. Hen's favorite flowerpot falls to the floor and smashes into a hundred broken pieces.

Be Honest

When Ms. Hen steps back into her classroom, she sees the broken flowerpot. Her students watch her.

"Oh, dear!" sighs Ms. Hen. "My favorite flowerpot! How could this have happened?"

Everyone in the class shrugs and looks at one another. Their eyes all come to rest on Hippo. They think he should tell the truth about what happened.

While Ms. Hen cleans up the mess, Hippo feels very badly. Finally Hippo speaks up. "We were all so excited about winning our big kickball game," he says. "I guess nobody noticed the mess."

"A mess like this is very hard to miss," says Ms. Hen. "But I know how you all get excited about kickball."

Be Honest

Later, at the lunch table, everyone has something to say to Hippo.

"You should tell Ms. Hen the truth," says Puppy.

"She will understand," says Cat. "It was an accident."

Mouse reminds Hippo that a lie only makes things worse. "At first it was just an accident," she says. "Now it is an accident with a lie on top of it."

Hippo is afraid Ms. Hen will yell at him.

Pig has a different idea. "I would make something up," he says. "Tell Ms. Hen a story about how her flowerpot broke while everyone was playing kickball."

"That's not a good idea," says Puppy. "You'd just be adding a new lie on top of an old one."

"But this way, no one will get in trouble," says Pig.

Hippo returns to the classroom before lunchtime is over. He wants to tell the truth, but he doesn't want to get into trouble.

"Um, Ms. Hen," Hippo stutters.

"Come in, Hippo," says Ms. Hen. "Do you have something to tell me?"

Hippo opens his mouth to tell the truth, but another lie comes out instead. "When we were outside playing kickball, I saw a little airplane flying in loops over the playground," Hippo says. "Maybe it looped through the window and knocked over your flowerpot."

"That could be," Ms. Hen says. "Hippo, my flower needs a bigger pot to grow in. Why don't you stay after school to help me plant it again?"

Be Honest

While his friends play after school, Hippo rushes to the sandbox for his pail and shovel. He begins to dig up fresh soil for his teacher's flower.

Ms. Hen comes to meet Hippo in the schoolyard. "Thank you for the fresh soil," she says. "This bucket will make a great flowerpot. It won't break like the last one."

Again, Hippo starts to tell Ms. Hen the truth, but another lie comes out instead.

"I saw a giant around on the playground today," Hippo says. "The giant stomped all over the place and shook the ground with every step. Maybe all of that stomping and shaking knocked over your flowerpot."

"I would have noticed a giant," Ms. Hen says. "Something else must have knocked it over."

On the bus after school, Hippo sits next to Puppy. He tells Puppy what had happened.

"A giant!" Puppy says. "That is your biggest lie yet!"

"I wanted to tell her the truth," says Hippo, "but I was afraid she would be angry. Now it is much too late."

"It is never too late to tell the truth," Puppy says.

At home, Hippo is too worried to eat his dinner. Eating has never been a problem for Hippo!

Hippo has forgotten all about how he won the big kickball game. He doesn't feel like a big hero anymore. He feels like a big liar.

Later, Hippo gets into bed. He is so worried that he cannot sleep. He has never had trouble sleeping before. Finally, Hippo decides how to make everything better.

Be Honest

The next morning, Hippo gets to school before the rest of his friends. He goes straight to Ms. Hen's desk and says, "Ms. Hen, I have something to tell you. It was an accident. I didn't mean it. Then I lied."

"Slow down, Hippo," Ms. Hen says. "I'm listening."

With tears in his eyes, Hippo says he is sorry for breaking Ms. Hen's flowerpot. He is even more sorry for the lies that he told. "I didn't want to lie," he says, "but I didn't want to get into trouble, either. Now I know that telling the truth is the most important thing. I'll buy you a new flowerpot if you'd like."

"I'm happy with the one I have now," Ms. Hen says, pointing to Hippo's pail. "And I'm happy you learned an important lesson about telling the truth."

Be Honest

Let's Share

Illustrated by Lance Raichert

Let's Share

Bear and Hippo are having fun on the playground. They take turns going down the slide.

"After you," Hippo kindly says to Bear.

When they are finished sliding, the two friends run to the swing set.

"It's your turn to go first," Bear says politely.

Next, they share a ride on the seesaw. Bear goes up. Hippo goes down. Then, Hippo goes up and Bear goes down. Hippo and Bear make a good team.

Later, Hippo and Bear are digging in the sandbox. They see a green piece of paper sticking out of the sand. The two friends reach for it at the same time and pick it up. The piece of paper is a dollar bill!

Bear and Hippo's eyes light up!

"Wow!" they shout together. "A whole dollar!"

The two friends look around the playground. There is no one around, especially nobody who seems to be looking for a lost dollar bill.

But Bear and Hippo cannot celebrate yet. The money is not theirs. Neither of them has lost a dollar. Someone else must have lost it.

"Someone might need this money to buy food," Hippo worries.

"Then let's wait and see if anyone comes looking for it," says Bear.

The friends agree to wait. But who will hold onto their lucky discovery? Bear and Hippo wait on the playground for a very long time. Nobody comes looking for the dollar.

"Well, we've waited," Bear says. "Can we keep it?"

"Not yet," says Hippo. "Let's ask around."

Let's Share

Hippo and Bear set off across the playground. First, they find their friends Bunny and Cat.

"Have either of you lost anything?" Hippo asks.

Bunny and Cat look at each other. "Not that we know of," says Cat. "Why?"

"We found a dollar on the playground," says Bear.

"I know it's not my money," says Bunny.

"You're doing the right thing," says Cat. "Keep asking around. If you can't find anyone who lost a dollar, then it should belong to you."

Next, Bear and Hippo head back to the sandbox and find Pig and Mouse digging in the sand.

"Have you lost anything today?" Bear asks.

Pig and Mouse stop digging. "That depends," says Mouse. "What did you find?"

"We found a dollar on the playground," Hippo says. "It's not either of yours, is it?"

"You're lucky!" says Mouse. "We've been digging for treasure all day and all we've found is a bottle cap, a tin can, and a rubber band."

"What should we do?" asks Hippo.

"Give the dollar to me!" Mouse jokes.

"You've done enough," says Pig. "I think the dollar should belong to you now."

Let's Share

Bear agrees. He thinks they have done all they could to find who lost the dollar. Hippo disagrees. He thinks they can do more.

The two have asked everyone on the playground except Puppy, who is sitting at a picnic table.

"Have you lost anything, Puppy?" asks Hippo.

"I haven't," says Puppy.

"We found a dollar on the playground," Bear says.

"It's not mine," says Puppy.

"We've asked everyone," says Bear. "Nobody is looking for it. What should we do next?"

"Why don't you put up a sign?" says Puppy. "Wait one day. If no one comes to claim the dollar by tomorrow, then it belongs to you."

The next day, Bear and Hippo wait at a picnic table all day long. Many children and their parents visit the playground.

Most of them pass by Bear and Hippo's sign. Some stop to read it. But nobody claims the dollar.

Bear and Hippo argue about what to do next.

"Puppy said to wait one day," says Hippo.

"We've been here all day!" snaps Bear.

"But the day isn't over yet!" Hippo snaps back.

Bear and Hippo wait some more. They begin making plans for how they'll spend the dollar.

"I think I'll buy a giant candy bar!" says Bear.

"I'm going to save up for a new football!" Hippo says.

"It's starting to get dark," says Bear.

They stare at the dollar, thinking of how to spend it.

Let's Share

"Let's wait until tomorrow," says Hippo. "Someone might still come looking for it in the morning."

"I guess I can wait one more day," says Bear.

Hippo and Bear must decide what to do with the dollar until morning.

"I'll take it home," says Bear. "It will be safe with me."

"No way!" says Hippo. "You pass the candy store on your way home. The dollar is safer with me!"

Bear grabs one end of the dollar bill, while Hippo clutches the other. They tug so hard, they almost tear it.

Hippo has an idea that puts an end to their foolishness. "Why don't we hide it until tomorrow?"

To keep their treasure safe, the friends dig a hole on the playground and bury the dollar there.

The next morning, Puppy arrives at the playground to find Hippo and Bear shouting at one another.

Let's Share

"Hippo took my dollar!" yells Bear.

"No I didn't!" yells Hippo. "Bear took my dollar!"

Just then, Turtle walks by, waving a green dollar bill. "Look what I found!" he says. "A buried treasure!"

"Hey!" Bear and Hippo both shout. "That's mine!"

Puppy doesn't like to see his friends argue. "Only one person has the right to keep the dollar," he says, "and that's whoever lost it in the first place. And since nobody claimed it, I think the three of you should share it."

The three friends know Puppy is right. They decide to share, and take Puppy with them to the ice cream shop where they use the dollar to buy a sundae for four!

Goops

Written by Gelett Burgess
Illustrated by Tim Warren

What is a Goop?

Many years ago, a very polite man named Gelett Burgess wrote poems about naughty children who had poor manners.

Burgess named these silly creations "Goops."

By seeing how badly Goops behave, many children have learned to act nicely and use their very best manners.

Calling Names

Amanda Minnesinger James,
she called her sister
horrid names!

She called her brother
names, as well.
So bad I wouldn't
dare to tell!

It's shocking how
a Goop will act!
they have no manners,
that's a fact.

Talking While Eating

A Goop that always
makes me smile
is this one:
Marmaduke Argyll.

His mouth is full
from cheek to cheek.
Why should he then
attempt to speak.

It makes me smile,
but still, the fact is,
it is a most
unpleasant practice.

Whining

Whenever I hear
a puppy whine,
I always think
of Susie Klein.

I think of how
she hangs her head.
She doesn't speak —
she whines, instead!

Don't whine!
If you don't speak right out,
you are a Goop,
without a doubt!

Sticking Out Your Tongue

Do you ever
stick out your tongue,
like Isabel McClung?

No one but
a Goop would show
Rudeness such as that,
I know!

If you're good,
take my advice;
Please don't do it!
'Tisn't nice.

The Duty of the Strong

You who are the oldest,
you who are the tallest,
Don't you think you ought to help
the youngest and the smallest?

You who are the strongest,
you who are the quickest,
Don't you think you ought to help
the weakest and the sickest?

Never mind the trouble,
help them all you can.
Be a little woman!
Be a little man!

Goops

Rough and Rude

Elias Ethelbert McGuff,
Oh, he was rude and he was rough!

He used to pinch, he used to poke,
And called his rudeness just a joke.

What made him plague his playmates so?
He was a Goop and didn't know.

Leaving Things Around

When you're finished with your play,
Do you put your toys away?
Do you put away your hat,
And your coat, and things like that?
Or, are you like Esau Pound?
He's the Goop who leaves things 'round!

Teasing

How thoughtless was Roberto Lees!
For only thoughtless children tease.
He teased the little pussy cat,
He teased the puppy! Think of that!
He even teased his sister, too!
I think he was a Goop—don't you?

Ordering People

When John D. Pell wants something done,
Do you think he asks of anyone?
Oh, no! He orders someone to,
With "Get my hat!" or "Tie my shoe!"
The Goops all say rude things like these,
But you, of course, say, "If you please!"

Throwing Away Things

On the sidewalk Nancy Beal
Throws her old banana peel;
Throws her apple skin and cores,
Right in front of people's doors!
Isn't that a shocking trick?
Ask that Goop
To stop it, quick!

Goops

Selfish with Toys

A puppy, when he gets a bone,
Will keep it for himself alone.
So Bildad would not share his toys
Or lend them to the other boys.
He was a Goop, and so are you
If you are ever selfish, too!

Snatching Toys

No children ever like to play
With such a Goop as Jumbo Ray.
For he will snatch and grab the toys
Of all the little girls and boys.
Though Jumbo loves to fuss and fight,
You know, of course, it isn't right.

Goops

Lying and Fibbing

The queerest Goop in all the land
Was Annie Annabelle LeGrand;
She often said what wasn't true—
That's an awful thing to do!
But we are honest,
You and I,
We think it's wrong
To tell a lie!

Saying I Won't

"I won't!" says young Amelia Pratt.
"I won't do this! I won't do that!"

Now isn't "won't" the naughtiest word
That anyone has ever heard?

Now isn't that the rudest way
A Goop could answer?
I should say!

Cheating at Games

If you should ask why Rosamund
Eliza Puddingfoot was shunned,
I'd say, because she'd always cheat
In every game, so she could beat.
Only a Goop would act that way
And be dishonest in her play.

Snuffling and Sniffing

Annie Fanny Ruffle Riff,
Hear her snuffle! Hear her sniff!
Hear her sniffle! Hear her snuff!
See her—well, I've said enough.
You have seen her, I suppose,
The Goop who seldom blows her nose.

Goops

Not Going to Bed

I never saw Uriah Stead
When he was glad to go to bed.
There always was one thing to do
Before he could take off a shoe!
The little Goop was always late.
I hope you don't procrastinate!

The End